BLACK BEAUTY

Library of Congress Cataloging-in-Publication Data

Simpson, Anne, (date)
   Black Beauty / by Anna Sewell; retold by Anne Simpson;
illustrated by Tom La Padula.
      p.   cm.—(Troll illustrated classics)
   Summary: A horse in nineteenth-century England recounts his
experiences with both good and bad masters.
   ISBN 0-8167-2860-7 (lib. bdg.)   ISBN 0-8167-2861-5 (pbk.)
   1. Horses—Juvenile fiction.   [1. Horses—Fiction.]
I. La Padula, Tom, ill.   II. Sewell, Anna, 1820-1878.   Black Beauty.
III. Title.
PZ7.S60584Bl   1993
[Fic]—dc20   92-5805

BLACK BEAUTY

ANNA SEWELL

Retold by
Anne M. Simpson

Illustrated by
Tom LaPadula

Troll Associates

My first home was a large, rolling meadow, where I lived with my mother, a wise old horse named Duchess. I was a handsome colt, and because of my black coloring our master, Farmer Grey, called me Darkie.

There were other young horses in the meadow, too. Together we spent many hours galloping around the field, testing our speed. Sometimes our play turned rough, and we would bite and kick one another in fun.

One day, during an afternoon of wild play, I heard my mother whinny to me. "I want you to understand something," she said when I trotted over to her. "The other colts here are good colts, but they're fit only to haul carts. You are different; you're well bred and come from a line of fine horses. Your grandfather won many races, you know, and he'd hate to see you behaving like these other colts.

"For your own sake, I hope you will grow up gentle and good-tempered, and always do your best, no matter what."

My mother's words did not mean much to me then, but I often thought of them when I was older.

I spent four happy years in this meadow before Farmer Grey decided it was time for my breaking in. Breaking in! I knew what it meant for a horse to be broken in, and I was not looking forward to it. It signaled the end of play, and was the first step to becoming an adult horse.

There were many parts to my breaking in: learning to wear a saddle and bridle, and to carry someone on my back; wearing iron horseshoes; having a cart or carriage harnessed behind me; and always, always doing whatever was commanded of me. Farmer Grey was very gentle, but there was no getting around it—I didn't enjoy it.

Soon, though, the worst was over. To finish my training,

Farmer Grey would harness my mother and me to the carriage and take us for drives along pleasant country lanes. My mother was a good teacher, and I soon learned when I should go fast or slow, and what was expected of me.

During our drives, she often gave me advice that she thought would be helpful. We both knew that one day I would have to leave her. "There are many kinds of men," she told me. "Some are good, like Farmer Grey, but others are cruel. A horse never knows what his life will be like or who will buy him. But I hope that, wherever you go, you will always do your best and keep up your good name."

Shortly after this, I was bought by a man named Squire Gordon, and I left my mother and my first home behind.

Squire Gordon and his wife seemed very pleased with me. They were kind people, and I couldn't have asked for a better home. I was sure I would be happy here.

"What a beautiful horse!" cried the Gordons' two young daughters when they saw me.

"He has such a handsome face and lovely coloring," remarked Mrs. Gordon. "Why don't we call him Black Beauty?"

And so I was named.

Life at Birtwick Hall, Squire Gordon's estate, was pleasant and peaceful. John, the coachman, knew a lot about horses and treated them with skill and care. Squire Gordon kept several horses, but John seemed especially proud of me, and spent a lot of time grooming me until my coat shone and my mane and tail were as soft as silk. He also talked to me a great deal; and though I couldn't understand everything he said, I came to know what he meant, and what he expected me to do.

Two of the other horses became great friends of mine. One was a funny little pony named Merrylegs. In spite of his small size, he was full of energy, and his good temper made him a favorite of the squire's daughters.

Ginger, a tall chestnut mare, was quite another matter. From my very first day at Birtwick Hall, she was ornery and ill-tempered. She even accused me of being the reason she'd been moved to another stall. I had never met such an unpleasant horse and didn't think we would ever get along. But I began to understand Ginger a little better when Merrylegs told me about her.

"It's her own fault she was moved out of that stall," he said. "She's been biting and snapping at people since she got here."

"But why?" I asked. "The only things I ever bite are grass and hay. Why would she want to bite people?"

"I don't think she *wants* to," he replied. "It's just that she was treated very badly before she came here, and I don't think she knows any other way to react to people. But if there's one place that can turn her around, it's this one. I'm twelve years old now, and I've seen enough to know that there's no better place for a horse to live than

Birtwick Hall. The squire is kind, and John is wonderful with us. If Ginger doesn't start behaving soon, it's her own fault."

A few days after this, I was chosen to go out with Ginger in the carriage. I didn't know how she would react to being harnessed with me, but except for flattening her ears when she first saw me, she behaved very well. I soon found out that she was a hard worker who pulled her weight both uphill and down. Squire Gordon liked pairing us because we kept step so well, and after several outings Ginger and I became quite friendly.

One day, when she and I stood alone in the paddock, we started talking about our early lives. It was then that I finally understood what Merrylegs had told me.

"If I'd had your type of upbringing, I'm sure I'd be as good-tempered as you are," Ginger said. "But mine was hard. No one was ever kind to me.

"It started when I was young, and groups of boys would come into our field and throw stones at us to make us gallop. I began to think of people as the enemy, and no one has ever given me a reason to think differently."

"What about your breaking in?" I asked.

"Oh, *that*," she said, with a toss of her head. "Well, I wasn't given much of a choice about it, was I? I wasn't broken in gently, like you. I was *forced* to wear a bit and bridle, *forced* to wear a saddle and carry someone on my back—and if I didn't like it I was whipped.

"Oh, I know I've got a reputation as a troublemaker, but I only get angry and kick when I'm not treated well. I'm willing to work hard, but what right does anyone have to treat me cruelly?"

I had to agree with her, and our conversation only made me more grateful for the pleasant years I'd spent with my mother in Farmer Grey's meadow.

11

Time passed quickly at Birtwick Hall. I was treated well, and looked forward to the days when Ginger and I were harnessed to the carriage to take the squire or his wife for a drive.

One morning in late autumn, John hitched me to the dogcart so I could drive Squire Gordon to town on business. It had rained heavily the night before, and there was a strong wind blowing. We had a long way to travel, but everything went smoothly until we came to a low, wooden bridge.

"The river is rising fast," warned the man at the tollgate. "I think tonight will be very bad indeed."

We made it safely into town, where I was given food and allowed to rest. But as the squire's business took longer than expected, we did not start out for home until very late in the afternoon. By then, the wind was whipping quite fiercely.

I had never been out in such a storm, and I was nervous about the weather. But I remembered what my mother had said about always doing my best, and so I trotted on. Suddenly, with a frightening *crack!*, a huge oak tree came crashing down across the road in front of me. I stopped in my tracks, terrified.

"That was a close call!" said the squire. I could tell he was shaken, too. "And how will we get to the bridge now?"

"We'll have to double back and take a longer road, Squire," replied John. "It will make us late, but Beauty doesn't seem tired yet."

By the time we reached the bridge, it was almost dark. The wind was still blowing fiercely, and I could hear the river rushing madly below. I started to cross the bridge, but as soon as my feet touched the planks I knew that something was wrong. I stopped and would go no further.

13

"Go on, Beauty," called the squire. But I didn't move. John gave me a touch of his whip, but I refused to stir.

"Something's wrong, sir," said John. He leaped out of the cart and tried to lead me forward. "Come on, Beauty! What's the matter?"

How I wished I could speak! But there was no way for me to tell them that the bridge was unsafe. I could only stand there and not move a step.

Just then we saw a lantern being waved about frantically on the other side. The man at the tollgate cried out, "You there, stop! Stop, I say! The bridge is broken in the middle— part of it has washed away! If you go any further, you'll end up in the river!"

"What!" exclaimed the squire.

"Oh, thank you, Beauty!" said John, and gave me a loving pat on the nose. "I *knew* something had to be wrong for you to act that way."

Our journey home was a long one. When we finally reached Birtwick Hall, Mrs. Gordon ran out of the house, crying, "Oh, thank goodness you're safe! It's so late— I've been imagining all sorts of things. Did you have an accident?"

"No, my dear," the squire replied. "But we might not be here right now if it wasn't for Black Beauty."

John led me to my stall, where he was generous with food and my bed of straw. I was glad, for by then I was very tired.

Not long after the incident at the bridge, Squire Gordon and his wife decided to visit some friends. The journey would take nearly two days, and Ginger and I were chosen to pull the carriage.

The first day of travel was long, but pleasant enough. By now, Ginger and I were quite fond of each other, and we took advantage of any long, flat stretches of open road to talk and share stories. It reminded me of the times I had been harnessed with my mother at Farmer Grey's.

By sundown we reached the town where we would spend the night. Ginger and I were glad to have our harnesses unbuckled. We were taken to a hotel stable, where a quick, efficient hostler rubbed us down and fed us.

Later in the evening, when I was almost asleep, a young man with a pipe came in to gossip with the hostler, who was caring for a newly arrived horse. "Would you do me a favor?" I heard the hostler ask. "Run up into the loft and bring down some hay for this stall. Just make sure you put down your pipe." After that, I stayed awake just long enough to hear the young man walk across the loft overhead.

I don't know how long I slept, but I woke up quite suddenly. It was completely dark. The air was thick and hard to breathe, and I heard Ginger coughing. There were strange sounds coming from the loft—a soft rushing, like the wind, then crackling and snapping. I didn't know what was happening, but I began to tremble all over. By now the other horses were awake, too; some were pulling at their halters, others were stamping nervously.

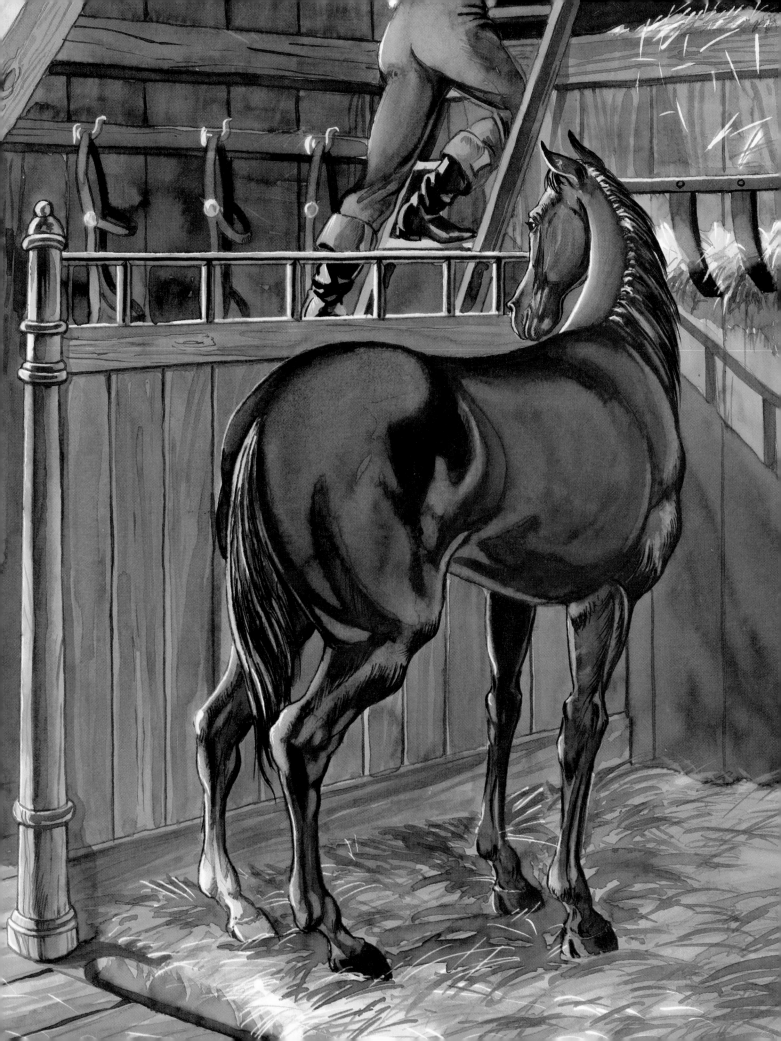

After what seemed like an eternity, the hostler came running into the stable. He untied some horses and tried to lead them out, but he was so frightened himself that he only added to our panic. The horses refused to move.

"Come on, you silly beasts!" he muttered. "You've got to get out before it's too late!"

After failing to coax several horses out of the stable, the hostler tried to drag me out of my stall, but I wouldn't move. How could I? Danger seemed to be everywhere, and there was no one I could trust.

"Come on, come on!" he cried, but when he saw it was no use he ran out of the stable.

The crackling sound grew louder, and I could see red lights flickering on the far wall. Cries of "Fire! Fire!" came from outside. Flames leaped out of the loft, and the rushing noise became a violent, thundering roar.

I was nearly crazed with fear. Then I heard John's voice, quiet and cheerful, as though nothing was wrong. "Come, my pretties, we must be off now, so wake up and come along." Here was someone I could trust!

He came to my stall first. "Come, Beauty, on with your bridle, and we'll soon be out of this mess." His soft voice was calm and soothing—just what I needed in my panic— and I gladly obeyed him. In no time, my bridle was on. Then he took off his scarf, tied it over my eyes, and with some gentle patting and coaxing led me out of the stable.

In the safety of the yard, he slipped the scarf off my eyes and shouted, ''Here, someone! Take this horse while I go back for the other.''

Ginger! I whinnied frantically to my friend as I watched John run back into the burning stable.

What a commotion there was in the stable yard! People and horses were everywhere, and frantic whinnies mixed with excited voices as the fire grew worse. The tremendous roar of the flames engulfing the stable thundered over all the noise from the yard. I kept my eyes on the stable door, wishing that John would bring Ginger out. Suddenly there was a loud crash from inside. I feared the worst—then, seconds later, I saw John lead Ginger from the burning building!

"Make way for the fire engine! Stand back!" someone shouted. The next thing I knew, there was a deafening clatter as two large horses pulling a heavy fire engine dashed into the yard.

Ginger and I were led away to a nearby stable, where we gladly got some rest after our terrible fright. She told me later that if she hadn't heard me whinnying from the stable yard, she wouldn't have had the courage to follow John outside.

The next morning, we heard John and the hostler talking. No one knew for sure how the fire had started, but it was thought that the man with the pipe was the cause. "I'll say one thing, my friend," the hostler said. "Your horses know who they can trust. It's one of the hardest things in the world to get horses out of a stable when there's a fire or a flood."

The hostler was right—Ginger and I did know who to trust. It was lucky for both of us that John was there that night.

Several months went by. It was spring, and life at Birtwick Hall was peaceful and pleasant. Ginger, Merrylegs, and I laughed and chatted in the paddock, and looked forward to the months of warmer weather.

Then one night I was roused from my sleep by the clanging of the stable bell. The stable door flew open, and John ran in, crying, "Wake up, Beauty, you must run your fastest tonight!"

Before I could even think, he had the saddle on my back and a bridle on my head. We took a quick trot to the main house, where the squire was anxiously waiting.

"Hurry, John! You're riding for Mrs. Gordon's life tonight! Tell Dr. White he must get here quickly—then let Beauty rest at the inn, and be back as soon as you can. There's not a moment to lose!"

With that, we were off. "Now, Beauty, do your best," John told me urgently, and so I did. For eight miles— through thick woods, uphill, downhill—I galloped as fast as I could, needing neither whip nor spur.

The church clock struck three as we pulled up at Dr. White's house. John leaped off my back and pounded on the door.

An upstairs window was thrown open. "What do you want?" asked Dr. White.

"Mrs. Gordon is very ill, sir; Squire wants you to come at once. He thinks she will die if you cannot get there."

In a flash, the doctor was dressed and at the door. "There's a problem—my horse has gone lame. Can I take yours?"

John hesitated, looking at me. "He's galloped nearly all the way here, sir, and I'm sure he needs rest. But if any horse can get you there in time, Beauty's the one. Take him—I'll walk."

And so the doctor and I galloped off. He was much heavier than John, and not as good a rider. But I knew that Mrs. Gordon's life was at stake, and that was all that mattered. Exhausted as I was, I raced back the way I had come.

It was just getting light when we reached Birtwick Hall. Little Joe Green, the Squire's newest stable boy, led me to my stall while the doctor hurried into the house. My legs shook after my grueling run, and my coat was wet all over. I stood, exhausted and panting heavily, as Joe ran to get some water.

Joe loved horses very much, but this was his first job in a stable, and he had a lot to learn. I know he only did what he thought was best for me, but although he rubbed down my legs and chest, he did not know enough to cover me with warm blankets. And he gave me plenty of cold water to drink, which tasted wonderful but wasn't good for me.

Joe left the stable, thinking I was well taken care of. Soon I began to tremble with the cold. How I wished for a blanket! My legs and chest ached, but all I could do was lie there, shivering. How long would it be before someone came in? John had eight long miles to walk, and Joe had gone back to his quarters.

I lay there for a very long time. When John finally walked in, I gave a low moan, for I was in great pain. He ran to my side, and seemed to know immediately what was wrong.

"That stupid boy!" he muttered. "No blanket for the horse, and he probably gave him cold water, too." He quickly covered me with warm blankets and gave me some hot water.

I was very ill with fever. My lungs were infected, too, so that it hurt even to breathe. John came and nursed me night and day. The horse doctor paid a visit every morning.

Squire Gordon often came to see how I was doing. "Poor Beauty. Do you know you saved your mistress's life? Yes, Beauty, you did—any longer and it would have been too late for her."

I was very glad to hear it.

Joe spent many hours by my side, too. He seemed very sad, and often told me how sorry he was for making me ill. I wanted to tell him I knew he'd only been doing his best, but there was no way I could.

This was a hard time for me; there were many moments when I thought I would die, and I believe they all thought so, too. But in time, with good care, my spirits and my health returned. Once again, I was able to join Ginger and Merrylegs in the paddock, and eventually I was well enough to be harnessed to the carriage and drive the Gordons about. Everyone was pleased at my recovery, and I was glad to be feeling good again.

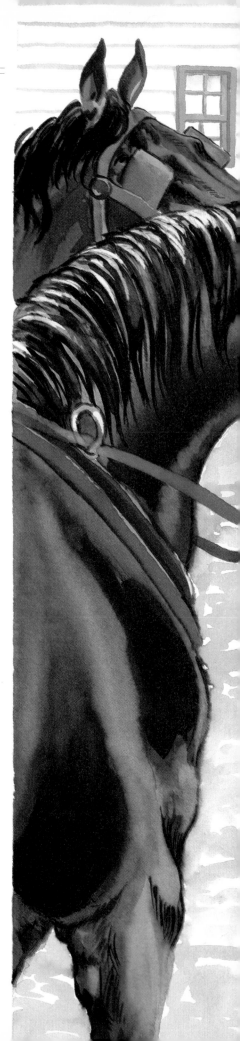

We didn't know it then, but changes were coming to Birtwick Hall. My time with the Gordons was drawing to an end. Although there were no more frantic runs to the doctor, Mrs. Gordon was still very ill. Finally, Dr. White advised her to leave the country and move to a warmer climate.

"I hate to sell off the horses and the house," Squire Gordon told John, "but there's nothing else I can do."

Sadness fell over the entire household. No one wanted to leave the Gordons or Birtwick Hall, but it couldn't be helped. Squire Gordon reluctantly made arrangements to move his family.

The day finally came when Ginger and I drove the Gordons to the train station for the last time. It was a sad time indeed.

"Good-bye, Black Beauty," the squire's wife whispered to me. "I shall never forget what you did for me." The squire and the little girls patted Ginger and me, and whispered kind words in our ears. Then they were gone.

Back at the stable, Ginger, Merrylegs, and I had a worried discussion. None of us knew where our next home would be. What would become of us? Until now, I had only known kind people and good care. What would my next owner be like?

I got my answer the next morning, as John hitched Ginger and me to the carriage. Happily, we'd both been sold to a wealthy earl who owned a large country estate several miles away. Merrylegs had been given to an old friend of the Gordons, on the condition that he never be sold. I hated saying good-bye to the friendly pony, for I knew I would never see him again. But Ginger and I had to leave for our new home.

The estate was called Earlshall Park, and it was a fine establishment. The main house was large and well kept, and there were many comfortable stables. For the most part, Ginger and I were content. We were well fed, and looked after by grooms who knew their business. But as Ginger and I often commented to each other, there was something missing—the feeling that the people around us were our friends.

Soon we discovered that one person at Earlshall Park was definitely *not* our friend. The earl's wife was a stern-looking woman with a harsh voice. Ginger and I were often harnessed to the carriage so that she could be driven to other estates for tea. But she was a fashion-conscious woman, and in keeping with the style of the day ordered the coachman to place Ginger and me in a bearing rein whenever we drove the carriage. I had never worn this type of rein, because Squire Gordon had thought it was cruel. But Ginger knew what it was like, and was not happy about wearing one. In a matter of days, I understood why.

One afternoon, Ginger and I were harnessed to the carriage as usual. But suddenly our reins were pulled so tight that our heads were unable to move up or down. This was uncomfortable, and it made it impossible for us to use all our strength. I felt shooting pains go through my back and legs when we tried to go uphill.

"Now you see what I've been talking about," Ginger said, when we returned to the stable. "Today wasn't too bad. But if they decide to make our reins any tighter, they'd better watch out! I promise you, I won't take it."

Unfortunately, as Ginger feared, our reins got tighter each day. I began to dread being put into the harness, although I made the best of it and didn't complain. Ginger didn't say much, but I knew she was getting restless.

After many weeks of this, the earl's wife came out one day, took one look at Ginger and me, and reprimanded the coachman. "Really, York, I've had enough of this nonsense. These horses aren't fit to be seen. Raise their heads at once!"

The man reluctantly drew back my head, fixing the reins so tight it was almost unbearable. Ginger saw what was coming, and as the groom walked around to her she reared up suddenly and knocked him over. Several servants ran to hold her, but she just kept rearing and kicking until she tired herself out.

I was led back to the stable, and Ginger was brought in soon afterward. She was never put into the carriage harness again.

I was still considered to be a trustworthy, good-tempered horse, so as a reward I still drove the earl's wife—harnessed with the bearing rein. For four long months I suffered this way, growing more irritable and worn out each day. But I remembered my mother's advice and continued to do the best I could.

I didn't know how much longer I could endure this. Luckily, the Earl and his family left Earlshall Park for an extended visit. There was no need for the bearing rein then, and the horses that were left behind were used only for riding.

The head groom, Reuben Smith, was left in charge of the stables. He was a well-liked man who knew horses thoroughly. One day, he rode me into town to attend to some business. I was left in the care of a hostler at an inn.

Somewhere along the journey, a nail had started to loosen in one of my front horseshoes. The hostler didn't notice it until later in the day. When Reuben finally returned for me, it was well into the evening, and he was in a terrible mood.

"Shall I fix this nail for you, sir?" asked the hostler.

"No, no," Reuben replied coldly. "The horse will be fine until we get home."

I was surprised, for Reuben was usually very careful about things like that. But there was nothing I could do. I was saddled up, and we set off for Earlshall Park.

I don't know why Reuben was in such a temper that night, but he was not the man I knew. Although I galloped at full speed, he gave me frequent cuts of his whip. The roads were very stony, too, so my shoe became looser and looser. Soon it came off entirely.

Normally, Reuben would have noticed the change in

my pace immediately. But because he was in such a terrible mood, I was forced to run my fastest while sharp stones cut into my split, shoeless hoof.

I carried on as long as I could, but finally the pain was too great for me to even stand. I stumbled, and fell to my knees. Reuben was flung off my back, and landed with great force on the sharp stones. He groaned and made an effort to rise, then lay completely still.

I limped to the side of the road, onto the soft grass, and waited for someone—anyone—to approach. But all was quiet, and I could only stand there, helpless to do anything for Reuben or myself.

Hours passed. Finally, two men appeared on horseback and stopped to help. At first they thought I had been careless and stumbled, but when they saw my broken hoof and damaged knees they seemed to understand what had happened. Poor Reuben, though, paid the heaviest price of all—he was dead by the time the men arrived.

In time, my broken knees healed, but the horse doctor said my scars would never fade. I was judged to be unfit for the earl's stables, and put up for sale. Ginger was upset by the news. "You're my only friend, and we'll probably never see each other again," she told me.

On the day I left, we neighed sadly to each other until I could no longer hear her.

My new master owned a stable full of horses and carriages that he rented out to people. Until now, I had always been driven by people who knew about horses. But my new home was different. Here I was driven by whoever had the money to pay for me.

It was hard work, and I became familiar with many different types of people. There were those who held the reins with such savage tightness that they made my mouth sore. Others were careless, and held the reins so slack that they had absolutely no control over me.

But probably the worst drivers were those who looked upon horses as machines. It made no difference to these drivers how heavy my load was, whether the road was rocky or muddy, or even if I was going uphill or down— they were determined to get their money's worth from me, no matter what it took. And so, even when I was struggling to do my best, they would cut me with their whips and call me a lazy beast.

This was my home for many months. Then I was brought to a horse fair to be sold. There were horses of every description at the fair—some young and handsome; others, like me, who were well-bred, but had seen better days; and, in the background, some sad-looking animals who had suffered from hard work and abuse.

I was poked and prodded by many people. They pulled my mouth open, checked my legs, and watched me trot so they could see my pace. But in the end, my scarred knees prevented me from being sold. People were afraid I would stumble and fall easily, and there was no way for me to explain what had really happened.

Toward the end of the day, just when I was wondering if I would ever have a new home, two men approached the salesman. They couldn't have been more different. The first was very loud and unpleasant, and reminded me of the kinds of people I had put up with as a hired horse. I hoped he would not buy me.

The other, though, had a kind voice and spoke gently. I could tell by the way he handled me that he knew a lot about horses, and I was sure I would be happy with him.

The two began bargaining for me. I feared that the unpleasant man would get me, for he seemed to have more money. But the man with the kind voice made the final offer. And with the salesman's "Sold!" my life as a London cab horse began.

Up and down crowded city streets in all kinds of weather, pulling a cab filled with people and their belongings—that is the life of a London cab horse. My new owner's name was Jerry, and although the work wasn't easy, I always did my best to please him. I knew I was lucky to be owned by someone so kind, for Jerry and his family treated me well. All around me I saw horses whose drivers treated them badly, and it made me sad.

One day, while Jerry and I waited at the curb for a fare, a shabby old cab drove up beside us. The horse looked worn out; her bones showed through her dull coat, and her knees were knuckled over. I was shocked to see such a hopeless look in her eyes. Just as I was wondering where I had seen the horse before, she said, "Black Beauty! Is that you?"

And then I knew. "Ginger!" I cried. "What has happened to you?"

She coughed a little, then said, "I've had a hard time of it since I last saw you. First one owner, then another, and another . . . I've lost count of how many. None of them treated me well. Now I work for a man who hires out his cabs to anyone with the money to rent them. I'm being worked until I drop, with never a day's rest."

I looked at her, and saw that all the spirit and life was gone; only suffering remained. "You used to stand up for yourself when you were mistreated," I protested.

"What's the use? Our owners still treat us just as they like. Where has all my fighting gotten me in the end? I'm just a broken-down cab horse."

I couldn't think of anything to say, so I nuzzled my nose gently against hers.

She nuzzled me back. "I'm glad to see you looking well, though, Beauty. You know, you're the only friend I ever had."

Just then, her driver tugged at the reins and drove her away, leaving me very sad. I never saw Ginger again.

I hoped that my pleasant life would continue, but it was not to be. Around New Year's Eve, our long hours in the bitter cold took their toll on Jerry, and he became very ill with bronchitis. When the children came to clean and feed me, I learned that Jerry was confined to his bed. It was a sad time for everyone. I hadn't been as happy with an owner since I left Squire Gordon's estate, and I hoped that Jerry would soon recover.

Finally, there was good news—Jerry was improving, and expected to get well. But the family had decided to sell the cab and me and move to the country. Once again, I was faced with the prospect of a new owner, a new life. But I was also older now, and I knew that my chances of finding such a happy home again were not good.

I never saw Jerry again; when I left the stable for the last time, he was still not well enough to go outside. But his family came out to wish me a tearful farewell.

"Good-bye!" said Jerry's wife as she kissed my nose. "We'll miss you and think of you often. How I wish we could take you with us!"

And so it was that I left another home I loved.

After I left Jerry and his family, I went from owner to owner, always being overworked, before I again became a London cab horse. But if I thought that cab work had been difficult before, I was about to find out just how bad it could be.

My new owner was completely different from Jerry; he was a harsh, cruel man who owned a large fleet of cabs. He had a temper that he took out on his drivers, who in turn took their anger out on the horses. I worked hard seven days a week, with little rest. And I never complained, although my driver was a horrible man.

"Hurry up, will you, you stupid beast!" he would bellow as I strained to move a heavy load up a steep hill. "You're not moving fast enough!" And he would crack his whip, often until he drew blood.

I was miserable, and could only think of my last meeting with Ginger. She had been right—we *were* powerless against our owners.

One day, a mother and father with two young children approached our cab at the train station. They had an enormous amount of luggage, and I groaned to myself when I saw it. The little girl ran up to me while the baggage was being loaded.

"Papa, look!" she cried. "This poor horse is too weak to carry us and all our bags. Can't we take two cabs?"

"Oh, don't you worry, missy," said my driver. "This horse is strong enough."

Box after heavy box was placed on top of the cab. "Please, Papa," the girl begged, as the springs of the cab sank under the weight. "The horse can't stand it—it's cruel!"

"Don't be silly, Grace," her father replied. "This driver

knows his own horse. If he says the beast can handle it, he can!''

Finally, all the baggage was loaded. With a slash of his whip, my driver took me out of the station. The load was as heavy as I had feared, and I hadn't eaten or rested since early morning, but I did my best. I managed all right until we came to a hill.

''Come on!'' yelled the driver, putting his whip to use.

Suddenly my feet slipped from under me, and I fell on my side. I couldn't move—I thought I was dying. All around me I heard loud, angry voices—and, through all the commotion, the little girl's cry. ''See, Papa! That poor horse. It's all our fault!''

''He's dead!'' someone cried out. ''He'll never get up.''

I lay there for what seemed like a very long time. Someone removed my bridle and threw cold water on my head. Then I felt a warm blanket cover me. Finally, a man with a soft voice patted me gently and helped me get up, and I was led to a nearby stable.

In the morning it was decided that I was no longer fit for cab work. I was fed well and rested for a week. Then I was taken to a horse fair to be sold again.

At this fair, I found myself in very different company. I was placed with the old, broken-down horses, where I stood patiently and hoped for the best. The day went very slowly. People didn't have much use for a horse who could no longer endure hard work. What would become of me?

Late in the afternoon, I saw a young boy strolling with an older man. The pair stopped at most of the horses they passed, even if only to give some poor, worn-out creature a friendly pat. Eventually they made their way to me.

"Oh, Grandpa, what a pretty horse he must have been!" said the boy when he saw me. "Look what a handsome face he has—and such beautiful coloring!"

"Yes, my boy," agreed the man. "He must have been something. I'd say this horse has seen better days." He patted my neck gently.

"Grandpa, remember Ladybird? She was an old horse, and you made her young again. Why don't you try with this one? He's so beautiful, and I'm sure he just needs some good food and rest and—"

"Willie, I can't make all old horses young," the man said gently, laughing.

Just then the salesman broke in. "Why, sir, this horse really isn't old at all. He's just had a hard time of it recently. I think the young man here is right—plenty of food and rest, and this fellow will be in fine shape again."

I was glad the salesman spoke, because the old gentleman started to look me over more thoroughly. He seemed pleased with what he found, and his touch was so gentle—the first bit of real kindness I'd had in months—that I responded by nuzzling him and letting out a soft whinny.

"See, Grandpa, he *wants* to come home with us!" cried the boy. "Oh, please, won't you take him? I just know you can help him."

The boy continued to plead with his grandfather, and to my delight he convinced him. I was now the property of Mr. Thoroughgood and his grandson Willie.

I don't know exactly what Mr. Thoroughgood did for that other horse, but I can only say that his treatment of me was just what I needed. I was given the run of a large, open meadow, and the food and rest I'd been longing for. Just being out of the crowded, bustling city was cure enough; I had no careless drivers, no more whips or insults. Before long, my spirits and health revived. I was beginning to feel young again.

Willie had been put in charge of my care, and he took his duties seriously. Each day, no matter what the weather was like, he came to visit me. He always had a treat and some encouraging words. Mr. Thoroughgood came by, too, and I could tell he was happy with my progress.

"Willie," he said one day, "you were right about this horse. A little kind treatment was all he needed. Just look at him—he really seems younger. The next thing is to give him some light work, and soon he'll be as good as new."

I was harnessed to a lightweight carriage, and Mr. Thoroughgood and Willie took me for a drive. My legs were no longer stiff, and I could do the work quite easily. The two seemed delighted, and I began to look forward to these pleasant journeys.

Several months later, when the weather was warm, Mr. Thoroughgood said, "Even-tempered, good paces—Willie, this horse is a gem. We must now try to find a good, quiet home for him where he will be valued."

One day I was cleaned and groomed with such extraordinary care that I knew something special was about to happen. Even my harness received extra polish! I was hitched to the chaise, where Willie and his grandfather were waiting. The boy seemed anxious, but he didn't say anything.

"I hope the ladies like him," said Mr. Thoroughgood. "It seems a perfect match all around."

We drove several miles over quiet country roads until we came to a pretty house set on lush, sweeping grounds. Willie rang the bell, and in a moment three older women came out to look at me.

"Well, ladies, what do you think?" asked Mr. Thoroughgood. "I can tell you, a gentler, more willing horse would be hard to find."

"He certainly is a beauty," said one with a smile.

"Yes," agreed another. "But what about his knees? He's obviously fallen once—what's to stop him from stumbling again?"

"I don't know the exact circumstances of the horse's fall," the old man replied, "and I certainly don't want to influence you. But many fine horses have had their knees broken due to careless drivers, and from what I've seen of this one, I'd say that was the case."

Now the third lady spoke. "You've been a trusted advisor to us about our horses, Mr. Thoroughgood, and we value your recommendation highly. But I would like our coachman to have a look at him first."

"Of course," Mr. Thoroughgood said. "Willie, why don't you run to the stables and fetch the coachman? There's a good lad."

Willie ran off, and returned a few minutes later with a handsome young man. "Hello there, Mr. Thoroughgood," the coachman said. "So this is the horse you've told us about?" He smiled when he saw me, then frowned and bent down to look at my knees. "I didn't think, sir, that you would recommend my ladies buy a horse with ruined knees, no matter how pretty he is."

"I know what you're thinking," said Mr. Thoroughgood, "but I can assure you that he's as safe as any— "

"Wait a minute!" the coachman suddenly broke in. "I once knew a horse that looked exactly like this one. I wonder . . ." He began to examine me closely. "White star on forehead, one white foot, same height . . . And here, in the middle of his back, that little patch of white hair—it *must* be Black Beauty!"

The others looked puzzled. "Black Beauty?" Mr. Thoroughgood asked.

The young man laughed and patted me gently. "Oh, Beauty, do you remember me? I'm Joe Green, the stable boy who almost killed you so many years ago."

Black Beauty! It had been a long time since I had been called by that name. I certainly didn't recognize Joe now,

for he was no longer the young boy I had known. But I was so happy to have a friend that I gave him a gentle nuzzle.

"You must have seen some hard times, Beauty," he said. "I wonder who the rascal was that broke your knees. Well, I intend to see to it that you have only good times now. Ladies, I beg you to take Mr. Thoroughgood's advice. You'll never see a finer horse."

Then Joe told everyone that he was sure I was Squire Gordon's old Black Beauty. The ladies smiled, and I knew I'd found a happy home at last.

I have now lived a whole year in this wonderful place. Joe takes special care of me, and Willie visits whenever he can. The ladies are quite pleased with me, and I enjoy driving them. Best of all, they have promised never to sell me. I have reached my final home at last, and it is a happy one; so here my story ends.

But there are times in the early morning, before I'm fully awake, when I stand in the green meadow and dream I'm back at Squire Gordon's, talking with Ginger and Merrylegs under a shady tree.